ANIMAL BAND

Christopher S. Jennings

STERLING

New York / London

Library of Congress Cataloging-in-Publication Data
Jennings, C. S.
Animal band / by Christopher S. Jennings.
p. cm.
Summary: As soon as the people go away, animals
gather to play together in an all-animal band.
ISBN-13: 978-1-4027-5307-7
ISBN-10: 1-4027-5307-1
[1. Bands (Music)—Fiction. 2. Animals—Fiction.
3. Stories in rhyme.] I. Title.
PZ8.3.J413Ani 2008
[E]—dc22
2007030750

10 9 8 7 6 5 4 3 2 1

Published by Sterling Publishing Co., Inc.
387 Park Avenue South, New York, NY 10016
Text and illustrations © 2007 by Christopher S. Jennings
The original illustrations for this book were created in pencil,
then scanned and colored digitally.
Designed by Scott Piehl

Distributed in Canada by Sterling Publishing
C/o Canadian Manda Group, 165 Dufferin Street
Toronto, Ontario, Canada M6K 3H6
Distributed in the United Kingdom by GMC Distribution Services
Castle Place, 166 High Street, Lewes, East Sussex, England BN7 1XU
Distributed in Australia by Capricorn Link (Australia) Pty. Ltd.
P.O. Box 704, Windsor, NSW 2756, Australia

Sterling ISBN-13: 978-1-4027-5307-7
        ISBN-10: 1-4027-5307-1

For information about custom editions, special sales, premium
and corporate purchases, please contact Sterling Special Sales
Department at 800-805-5489 or specialsales@sterlingpublishing.com.

For Rock.
Best cat.
EVER.

WALTER

THOMAS

ROCK

When the door's been locked
and the owner's away,
out come the instruments.

It's time to play!

Big Rock plays the trumpet—
a harmonica, too.

There's a knock on the door.
It's the gang from the zoo.

Open up the windows!
Open up the door!
Turn on the lights!
There's room for more!

So many choices.
Which one to pick?
Get something to play.
You have to be quick!

Make way for the lion.
He's one cool cat!

Get him something!
They say, "Oh, no!
There's nothing left
to strum or blow!"

They gather near.
The room is quiet.
Nobody breathes.
He's gonna try it!

He gives it a look.
He gives it a smell.
He reaches to tap
on its silvery bell.

A tone so quiet—
just one little sound . . .
then the Clatterazoo
starts moving around.

It's slow at first,
but it picks up speed.
It starts banging and thumping.
It sets the beat!

All the gang joins in.
They're the best in the land!
They play all night long.
They're the . . .

Animal Band!